ZANIB M

ILLUSTRATED
NASAYA MAFAR

PLANET OMAR

INCREDIBLE RESCUE MISSION

HODDER

HODDER CHILDREN'S BOOKS

First published in Great Britain in 2020 by Hodder & Stoughton

3 5 7 9 10 8 6 4

A CIP catalogue record for this book
is available from the British Library.

ISBN 978 1 444 95129 5

Printed and bound in Great Britain by
Clays Ltd, Elcograf S.p.A

The paper and board used in this book
are made from wood from responsible sources.

Hodder Children's Books
An imprint of
Hachette Children's Group
Part of Hodder & Stoughton
Carmelite House
50 Victoria Embankment
London, EC4Y 0DZ

An Hachette UK Company
www.hachette.co.uk

www.hachettechildrens.co.uk

This book is dedicated to

all the children who do what's right,

even when nobody is looking

Mrs HUTCHINSON

OMAR

I have a secret collection of buttons nobody knows about (except you, you obviously know now because I wrote it here)

Can lick my elbow (can you?)

Scared of pigeons >-<

I want to be on the first trip to Mars for people who aren't astronauts

BEEP.

BEEP,

BEEP,

B‰‰

CHAPTER 1

BEEEP!

That was my annoying alarm clock, waking me up for the first day of school after the holidays. I didn't want to get up because I had been sleeping until at least nine o'clock for the last two weeks, so seven o'clock felt like practically the

Middle of The NiGhT!

What was most annoying was that Mum had put it on the other side of the room, instead of on my bedside table, so I'd HAVE to get out of bed to turn off the beeps. Of course, I tried to be smart, so I threw my pillow at it. It was too heavy and fat or something, so it didn't get very far. I rummaged in my bedside drawer for something else to throw and found a squishy ball I had kept because it

smelled of delicious BUBBLE GUM.

I squinted at the clock and lifted the ball up ...

READY, AIM, THROW!

Yikes. Just then my sister Maryam was walking into the room saying,

'Turn that thing off, you lazy egg!'

GASP

Yep, you guessed it. She got hit straight in the nose. Lucky it was squishy or I would have got in LOADS of trouble.

Needless to say, the rest of

the morning did not go smoothly. Mum and Dad weren't very impressed and Maryam was super melodramatic about it, saying she wasn't ever going to talk to me again. Then my little brother Esa refused to put his coat on, which made us late, and everyone got even crosser. I was the only one in a good mood, because I couldn't wait to see my best friends, Charlie and Daniel.

They ran up to me in the playground and both gave me a slap on the back. A slap on the back is basically code for:

'Hey! I'm so happy to see you. I kind of missed you.'

The slap is less cheesy than actually saying it, SUPER OBVIOUSLY.

'Guess what?' said Daniel. 'My mum and dad finally got me a new bike! It's so cool. I can't wait to show it to you!'

'Ah. Lucky!' said Charlie.

'Yeah, the chain still keeps falling off when I ride mine,' I said.

'Isn't your dad really good at fixing stuff?' asked Daniel.

'Yeah, he is – I should ask him.

The only thing he can't fix is Maryam,'

I said. And we all laughed and agreed about that.

We couldn't stop chatting as we lined up in the playground for Mrs Hutchinson to collect

us. I had brought her a

chocolate cupcake

from the stash my neighbour Mrs Rogers

had brought over for us the day before. Mrs

Hutchinson is probably the nicest teacher ever.

I mean, duh, nobody on the entire planet would

give away one of their Mrs Rogers' cupcakes

to somebody they didn't like. I thought Mrs

Hutchinson deserved one, for the winks she

gave us at the right moments, for always being

fair when two kids got into a fight, and for the

fun way she taught us.

Before the holidays, we'd been doing a project about the universe and she told us about how some scientists believe there is life on

other planets. Basically, that means aliens, so Mrs Hutchinson got us to imagine what they might look like – it wasn't really like a lesson at all!

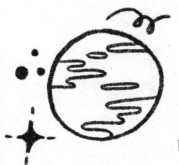

'Be careful, though,' she had said. 'They might be watching us. We don't want them to know we are on to them.'

But when a teacher came to bring us in, it wasn't Mrs Hutchinson.

It was someone
taller and thinner
and with way
less fun hair.

She had the kind of creases in her face that told me she had spent most of her life frowning and furrowing her eyebrows. Her clothes were grey and her shoes were POINTY. The way-less-fun hair was pulled so tightly

and so neatly into a bun at the back that I imagined she'd needed the help of a high-tech laser that detected any out-of-place hairs and zapped them down.

Daniel and Charlie looked at me with their question-mark eyebrows. Have you ever noticed that the eyebrows say the most about someone's feelings?

For example, Charlie has eyebrows to say:

EH? WHAT'S
GOING ON?

Most often seen when he is
doing one of his maths
problems.

WOW, THIS IS
SO FUN!

Most often seen when we
have discovered a new
game to play.

OMG, I'M
GOING TO DIE.

Most often seen when
a spider crawls up the
wall.

Anyway, back to the strange teacher.

Eerily, the only thing she said to us was, 'Follow me.' And she spun around on the sharpest heel I have ever seen and walked towards the school building.

CHAPTER 2

We piled into the classroom and went for our chairs.

'Who IS this?' whispered Daniel.

'Don't worry, it's probably nobody. Mrs Hutchinson's probably just sick or something and she'll be back tomorrow,' I said.

But just then, the new teacher said,

'I'm Mrs Crankshaw. I will be your teacher for the rest of the school year.'

She said those words from her mouth. But it felt like each word was a heavy, metal object, hitting me over the head.

I looked at Charlie. He had scared eyebrows. I wanted to put my arm around him.

Daniel was pinching my leg under the table.

'Daniel! Stop it. Ouch! What are you doing?'

'I'm pinching you to make sure I'm not dreaming.'

'YOU'RE SUPPOSED TO PINCH YOURSELF, SILLY!'

'You two at the back. Stop your nonsense,' said Mrs Crankshaw. 'That brings me to my first task – assigning you all to your new seats. From now on, you will not sit next to your chatty little friends, you will sit where I say.'

'She's not a nobody,' said Daniel.

'No,' I said. I looked down at the cupcake. It looked sad, too.

We had to
hold in all of our
questions and emotions
until break time. None of us
dared to put our hand up and ask
what had happened to Mrs Hutchinson.
Especially since my new seat neighbour,
Ellie, asked if she could do something as
innocent as get up and throw her pencil
sharpenings in the bin and she got
a LOOk that could
have made
Superman
poop his pants.

When we were released for break, Charlie, Daniel and I did some super-fast speed walking towards the exit, because we aren't allowed to run.

All of us buttoned up our lips until the fresh, cold outside air hit our faces and then Daniel practically exploded.

'Where's Mrs Hutchinson?' he wailed.

Charlie just stood there looking at us, not saying anything. He seemed to be in shock.

'So, it's not just for a day, she said she was our teacher *for the rest of the year!*' I said.

'But what happened to Mrs Hutchinson? Why would she just leave us?!' asked Daniel.

'I don't know. But we have to find out.'

I put my arm around Charlie, who still hadn't said anything. We couldn't lose Mrs Hutchinson *and* Charlie both in the same day!

Finally, Charlie spoke. 'Shall we ask one of the other teachers?'

'Good idea,' I said, already running towards the teacher on duty in the playground, Charlie and Daniel following close behind.

Mr Henry already had several children around him. He was telling one of them off, while another stood there crying and others watched.

We waited for him to finish shouting, then I said, 'Mr Henry, **where is Mrs Hutchinson?'**

The teacher looked in all four directions to figure out where the question was coming from. He didn't realise it was from me, because about six other kids were still staring at him.

'I don't know! In the toilets probably! Really, how should I know?' he said, rubbing his forehead as if it would make everyone go away.

Charlie tugged at my sleeve. 'Come on, this isn't working.'

We walked around the playground, not really saying much, which was fine by me, because my mind was busy imagining all the things that could have happened.

Maybe Mrs Hutchinson had too many of those very light cheese puffs she eats every lunchtime, and they made her weightless so she floated off into the clouds. Then I imagined that she somehow became invisible and was trying to get everyone's attention to help her come back down, but we just couldn't see her any more.

'Mrs Hutchinson! If you're there, throw a ball at us!' I said out loud.

'What?' said Charlie and Daniel. 'Have you gone nuts?'

I giggled.

'Worth a try...'

CHAPTER 3

On the way home, I told Mum all about the terrible disappearance of Mrs Hutchinson.

'I'm sure there's a reasonable explanation,' Mum said. 'They'll probably send us a letter about it.'

She was being very grown up, obviously because she is a grown up, but it was unhelpful and **SUPER BORING.**

I said, 'But, Mum! What if something has happened to her and we need to launch a rescue mission?'

Mum rolled her eyes at me and said, 'Hey, Siri, when do children stop overreacting to everything?'

Siri said, 'Here's what I found on the web.'

Siri was Mum's best friend these days.

I rolled my eyes
back at Mum

and figured Maryam might be more helpful.

Maryam was lying on her bed when I got

home, tapping away on her phone.

'WOW!

You actually remembered to knock.
You must want something.'

'Sort of. Mrs Hutchinson is gone and we

have a horrible teacher called Mrs Crankshaw

and Mum won't listen to me about it.'

'Oh. Where has she gone?'

'Well, that's the thing. Nobody knows.'

'Not right, Omar. Somebody knows.

You just have to find the somebody.'

'Where do I find the somebody?'

'Probably the staffroom. The staffroom is full of G⊕SSiP and SeCReTS. That's why kids aren't allowed in there.'

'Wow. Really?'

'Yes, really.'

'OK, thanks!'

'Whatever, beaver breath.'

I walked away, trying to smell my own breath, just to make sure.

I imagined what the staffroom looked like. None of my friends had ever seen it. But I guessed it would be dark and lined with dusty files, all containing terrible secrets. I imagined

the teachers taking their masks off when they
went in, and all of them were ACTUALLY
WITCHES, except Mrs Hutchinson ...
Maybe *that's* why they got rid of her?!

I ran downstairs to see if I could get Mum to listen to me again, but I got distracted by the bananas and crisps she'd put on the table for a snack. She said I could only have the crisps if I had a banana first, which is the only reason I had a banana, because I don't really like them unless they have the brown freckles all over, which means they are soft and sweet inside.

It turned out the snacks were a cheeky trap – like honey for a bear ... 'Please help Esa with his homework before you run off and disappear into your room, Omar,' Mum said, while I had my mouth full of banana.

'Mmmuuulm ...!'

I tried to wriggle out of it by saying, 'He never listens to me anyway.'

'Yes, he does.'

'No, he doesn't.'

'Yes, he does,' said Esa, which made me laugh.

I was only complaining because I wanted to get back to thinking about what we could do about Mrs Hutchinson. How long could a three-year-old's baby homework take? Plus, last time I helped him, Dad let me choose what he would cook for dinner, which was cool. I chose spaghetti bolognaise because, like I always say,

Dad's is the best.

'Come on, Esa,' I said. 'Let's do it in the living room.'

The homework was to colour in two shapes

that were the same in each row on a worksheet.

I could have done it in exactly 38 seconds

and, believe me, I was tempted to do it in a

scribbly way and just pretend that Esa did it,

but I was worried he would tell Mum and even

if he didn't, **Allah would super obviously know about it and He wouldn't be very proud of me.**

So, I sat with him for 30 minutes to help him

finish it, which is almost *ten times* slower than I

would have been. **Sheesh.**

In my head, I was imagining a new scientific

breakthrough in medicine which would make

toddlers faster at everything.

Everyone would want to buy that.

I would make millions. I decided I

might have to pay more attention

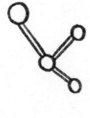

to what my scientist parents say

all the time, so I can get

super good at it and

make the medicine when

I grow up a bit.

As we were finishing, Dad came

home with his motorbike helmet still on his

head, which I always think makes him look a bit

like an alien.

Esa ran up and jumped into his arms. I gave

him a kiss on his helmet and he said,

'zorgle borg,

what a welcome is this! Take me to your leader,

Earthlings'.

We giggled at that, but it reminded me of

Mrs Hutchinson's alien lesson again, and my

tummy turned over thinking about going back

to school to Mrs Crankshaw.

CHAPTER 4

The next day, at school, we all sat in the seats Mrs Crankshaw had chosen for us. Charlie was near me, but Daniel was across the room. My seat was next to Ellie's. She was OK, but

definitely not as fun as sitting right next to one of my best friends. ☺

Maybe it would have been better if Charlie was further away, though, because having him close meant I still wanted to talk to him, but he

was too far away for me to whisper properly so
I got lots of CR⊗SS L👀KS
from Mrs Crankshaw.

She was teaching us about
how people lived in medieval
times. She wasn't making
history fun, like Mrs Hutchinson
would. It was as if she was *trying* to make it
boring. Maybe she had a 'making things boring'

super-villain power.

I bet she could even make Ferraris sound boring.

I wanted desperately to state the obvious
to Charlie, so we could both laugh about it,
but Mrs Crankshaw had her eyes on me. Ellie
suggested that if I wanted to say something
to Charlie, I could whisper it to her, and she
would whisper it to Sarah, who would whisper
it to Jason, who would whisper it to Charlie.

I agreed that was a good plan and whispered, **'This is boring.'**

I watched as the girls passed on my words to my best friend, who had understood what was going on and was grinning his toothy grin in anticipation.

When it finally got round to him, he said, 'What?

Chris is snoring??

No, he isn't!'

I face-palmed at the complete flop. If I was going to stop myself falling asleep, I needed to think more drastically ...

I shot my hand up to ask if I could go to the toilet. **I didn't need to pee, and before you think it, no I didn't need to p💩💩. I had a plan.**

Surprisingly, Mrs Crankshaw let me go.

I winked at Daniel on my way out.

I made my way down the hall, in the opposite direction to the toilets, looking over my shoulder in case Mrs Crankshaw was following me. I wondered what I would have done if I had turned around and seen her.

Pretended I was lost?

Or run? Or played dead?

(Hey, why not? It works for spiders!)

I arrived at my destination. You guessed it – the staffroom. I was hoping to bump into the *somebodies* who knew what was going on with Mrs Hutchinson. I was in luck, because one of the Year 2 teachers was walking towards me. She was walking the way Maryam does when she tries on a pair of Mum's heels for fun. I guessed it must be the first time this teacher had worn heels too.

I held my breath, in case she told me off for being there, but to my relief, she smiled and asked, 'How can I help you?'

'I, erm, wanted to ask if you know where Mrs Hutchinson is?'

Her smile vanished. 'Well, that's nosey, isn't it? Don't worry, if the school wants you to know, you will know,' she said. And then she walked into the staffroom and closed the door behind her without even looking at me.

Wow, that was secretive, I thought. *Maybe a bit too secretive. Something suspicious is going on.*

I started running back towards my classroom and then saw the 'no running' sign, so switched to speed-walking instead and then  realised nobody was around to tell me off, so switched to running again and then heard Dad's voice in my head saying, 'Do what's right, even if nobody is looking,'

so I sighed and switched back to speed-walking. It's hard work being good, sometimes.

I sat back down at my desk and quickly

scribbled a note to pass to Charlie:

CHAPTER 5

We were bursting to talk more at lunchtime, but we had to keep it in until we got into the playground after eating. That's because Sarah and Ellie were sitting right next to us in the canteen, and they were clearly in **EAVESDROPPING MODE.** Instead of talking to each other, they were just staring into space and smiling at each other now and then. **Could they be any more obvious?**

I wondered why they were so interested in us today. Usually they're chatting away about their own stuff …

I hoped they hadn't sneakily read the note I passed to Charlie! I figured if something was going on with Mrs Hutchinson, and the other teachers were in on it, then we had to keep it to ourselves until we knew more. It could be dangerous.

'Finally! We can talk!' I said, as soon as we left the canteen.

'*Talk* already! What do you mean Mrs Hutchinson is in trouble?' said Charlie, wiggling his eyebrows between excited and worried.

'What? When did this happen?' asked Daniel.

We told him I found out in medieval times,

which made us all laugh, even in this serious

situation.

'I hate being on the faraway table,

all the way in Narnia,'

complained Daniel. 'I'm going to be the last to

find everything out!'

'OR you'll be the first, but you won't be able to tell us.'

'Even worse! You know I can't keep anything in.'

'Yeah, we know,' said Charlie, fanning the air around his nose.

'What? It's not my fault,

I had beans for lunch ...'

We walked away from the smell, relocating in a more hidden spot behind a tree. I explained to my friends what the Year 2 teacher said to me. 'You know what that means, don't you? They are hiding something. All the teachers.

First, Mr Henry said that she was in the toilets and now this teacher is acting all suspicious and secretive.'

'**SeGRetY,**' corrected Charlie.

'I'm pretty sure it's secretive, but we can go with secrety.'

'So, what are we going to do?' said Daniel.

'I think we should launch a

SEARCH MISSION.

But not inside the school,' I said. 'Because the teachers are clearly in on it – or they would have told us what's happened to her.'

'What, like put missing posters up on lampposts?' asked Daniel.

'That's one idea, but we'll need to do more,' I said.

'Maybe we could ask

Lancelot Macintosh.

He's her uncle, remember?' suggested Charlie.

I did remember. Lancelot Macintosh is Mrs H's super-cool uncle, who drives a Ferrari without showing off, and who supported us in our save-the-mosque money-raising campaign.

'Yes! He should be the first one we talk to,' I said.

We made a plan to make missing posters, using a photo of Mrs Hutchinson from the wall at reception, where there was a photo of every member of staff in the school. Most of them weren't smiling in their pictures, they **were**

very serious, or even miserable,

except Mrs Hutchinson. She was smiling in

hers, as if she had just seen a **baby UNiCORn.**

Every time I looked at the wall, it made me want

to grab a sharpie and put smiles on everyone's

faces, the way Maryam and I draw funny hats

and moustaches on people in magazines.

'Daniel, would you mind bringing your phone in one day and taking a photo of her photo?'

I'm not allowed a phone of my own yet, even though lots of kids in my class have one, including Daniel. Mum and Dad say I can only get one when I am thirteen, which still feels like a million years away.

' I'm not allowed to use my phone at school...' started Daniel.

'Oh ... yeah ... hmmm.'

'But you know I'm going to do it anyway!'

he giggled

We giggled too, but I was hoping this mission wouldn't land any of us in trouble.

CHAPTER 6

After school, I went over to see our next-door

neighbour Mrs Rogers, because she always has

the best biscuits and listens to all my worries

without saying they are nothing to worry about.

'This is definitely

very suspicious,'

she said, after I finished telling her everything.

And I loved her for it. 'You could use The

Facebook to try to find her. Apparently, you can

write on The Facebook and the whole world can see it. My son John signed me up on it from his computer, which was nice, but I have to wait to use his computer again to look at it, because he didn't sign me up on mine.'

I pushed a giggle back into my mouth
because I didn't want Mrs Rogers to think I was
laughing at her.

'That's not how the internet works, Mrs
Rogers. You can sign into your Facebook account
from any computer, anywhere in the world.'

'Oh really? That is fascinating, isn't it?'

'Sort of,' I grinned.

'Well, the first step is to go and poke around
the area she lives in. Bet you'll find

LOTS OF CLUES

around there.'

'I know exactly which road she lives on,

because I saw her taking her grocery shopping in once, when Dad and I were driving past!'

'Fantastic. That makes things a lot easier. Get your dad to take you back, and then let me know how you get on,' said Mrs Rogers, with a wink. 'And say hi to your mum, tell her I haven't had a biryani in a while.'

BIRYANI

'Erm, we sent you some last weekend, Mrs Rogers.'

'Like I said, it's been too long!'

I giggled and promised I would ask Mum to make some more of her favourite Pakistani food. When we first moved in next door to Mrs Rogers, she hated the smell of our food cooking, but now that she's more part of our family, she gets excited by the smell, knowing what's going to hit her taste buds.

My dad told us that once, when he took a chickpea curry for lunch to his lab, all his colleagues thought that the smell was one of their experiments gone wrong, and he was super embarrassed until he let everyone taste it and they all went mad for the yummy flavour.

I walked the few steps back to my house, but I took my time because I heard a whizzing noise from up above. I looked up at the sky, where I could see nothing but clouds. But what was the sound? I imagined it was an alien spaceship, hiding behind the clouds. Which made me wonder ... what if Mrs H was in an alien spaceship? It wasn't impossible ... After all, she was the one who said there were aliens up there!

When I opened the front door,

Esa was unfolding all of the fresh

laundry Mum had just done and

flinging it across the room.

'It's sn❄wing!'

he grinned happily.

I jumped around trying to grab socks

and T-shirts from places high and

low. 'Stop it, Esa. Mum will

be super cross with you.'

Just then, Mum walked into the room with her cup of coffee in hand. **'For the love of rectangles!'** she blurted out.

Mum is so random.

She walked straight back out mumbling something about at least getting to finish a cup of coffee before it got cold.

I folded the laundry again, as well as I could. It's not as easy as it looks!

Then I used my very best puppy-dog eyes and asked Maryam if I could use her phone to call Charlie and Daniel.

'Get ready,' I told them.

'We're going on a <u>mission</u>, tomorrow after school, on our bikes...'

CHAPTER 7

The next day, we could barely focus on our already boring work in class, because we were dying for home time, when we would get on with our search for Mrs Hutchinson.

Mrs Crankshaw had to deal with her first class incident when Sarah tripped over Daniel's big boots and fell, hitting her head on the side of a desk. There was blood, right near her eyebrow. It wasn't pretty and **I was really worried about her,** especially because she was wailing very loudly.

But Mrs Crankshaw went over and looked at Sarah as if nothing had happened. As if she had no blood tricking down her cheek. 'OK. You can go to the welfare room,' she said. And *then* she put her hands over her ears, so she wouldn't be able to hear the crying.

It made me miss Mrs Hutchinson even more, who couldn't hide how worried she got when a kid hurt themselves, because

her springy curls would immediately lose their spring.

She would always send another child to the welfare room with the person who had hurt themselves, too, just to make sure they were OK on the way.

'Oh, she's cranky for sure,'

said Charlie in a whisper, looking at all of us near his table, the way he does when he makes a joke, like he's checking how funny it was.

We all laughed, which was a super bad idea because, as if by some witchy magic, our new teacher appeared out of nowhere, piercing us with her eyes.

'And what exactly is so funny over here?'
she demanded, looking at me. Probably because
I was the one who

LAUGHED
THE
LOUDEST.

'Nothing,' I said.

And before she spoke, I knew what she was
going to say. The same thing all adults on the
planet say when you say, 'nothing'.

'It's obviously not nothing. It's something.'

She crossed her arms and pursed her lips.

We all stared down at our hands in our laps, not daring to look up.

'Well, *nothing* can cost you your break time. So be careful.' She dropped this bomb as she spun around on her sharp heel and stormed off.

The class worked in silence for the rest of the day, but rumours were already starting to spread in the playground about Mrs Crankshaw being a

SUPER-VILLAIN who had

escaped from a
high-security jail

and disguised herself as a school teacher.

CHAPTER 8

After what seemed like for ever, we were finally

together on our bikes. Charlie, Daniel and me.

Dad had actually managed to sort out my chain

problem. We met at our usual spot,

which we had figured out was an equal distance

from all three of our homes. If you want to

know how we did that, I'll tell you. It was easy.

We all left our own houses on foot and counted

our steps on the way. Charlie had taken 215

steps, Daniel 189 and me 192. We noticed that

Charlie's steps are smaller, so it was actually

about the same distance. Dad said that the

whole thing **wasn't very °scientific**⊖

and he raised one eyebrow. It was the eyebrow

that told me I should know better because I am

the son of two scientists.

BUT COME ON,

sometimes even I can't be bothered to do

PERFECT SCIENCE.

'Right, guys,' I said, rubbing my hands together. 'First stop, Mrs Hutchinson's house. Follow me and be careful, it might be

A CRIME SCENE

that the police haven't discovered yet, so no touching anything. Except the doorbell. We'll have to touch the doorbell.'

'But what if we leave **fingeRpri🌀ts** and then later the police think we did it?!' said Charlie.

'Does everyone have gloves?' Daniel asked.

Luckily we'd all remembered to bring them. So, we put them on and sped off.

As we rode, Charlie said, 'She might just be at home. Maybe she just decided not to be our teacher any more.'

I thought about this in my head and said,

'No. Mrs Hutchinson would never, ever, do that.'

But my heart was beating at the thought of

her opening her front door. And when we got

there and I went to press the doorbell, my hand

was shaking.

BRRRRRING!

We waited. Charlie held on to the hood

of my jacket for comfort and Daniel held on

to Charlie's arm. Which made me imagine

myself as at the circus, being the person at

the bottom, that all the other people stand and

balance on. That person has to be the

STRONGEST,

to hold everyone up.
If I ran away now, we
would all run away. So,
I tried to remember to

*breathe
slowly.*

I conjured up my
imaginary dragon H_2O,
who breathes cool
steam. I don't very
often imagine him any
more, but I needed
him now, to help me
stay calm.

Nobody came to

the door, **which made me sad and happy all at once.** Sad, because that meant Mrs Hutchinson *was* missing. But happy because it meant that she didn't just decide to stop being our teacher.

We rang it another couple of times and waited, to be triple super sure. Then we peeked in through the letterbox.

There was a whole pile of post on the floor.

'You know what that means, don't you, guys?' I said quietly.

'She hasn't been home,' Charlie gasped.

'For *days*!' Daniel added.

YIKES!

Then we peered in through the front window, hoping to find more clues.

'Can anyone see anything?' Charlie asked, with his nose pressed up against the window.

'Errmm ... nooo ... not really ...' I said.

'What are we looking for, anyway?' said Daniel.

Just then, the freakiest creature ever pounced on to the windowsill from the inside and **hissed!**

All three of us jumped backwards on to the grass. Charlie practically jumped into Daniel's lap. **'Whaaaaaat was that?'** he shrieked.

'I don't know, I've never seen anything like it!' I said.

'I think it was just a cat ... *I think*,' said Daniel.

'But it wasn't furry!' Charlie was still shrieking. **'Or cute!'**

'Yeah, it was like just skin, yucky skin.' I grimaced.

'Like an **iNSiDe-ut cat!'** Charlie said.

'Guys, what if it's an alien? Trying to disguise itself as a cat, but it doesn't quite know what cats look like, or maybe its fur disguise feature is out of order?!' I said, thinking back to the spaceship I had imagined in the clouds.

Charlie and Daniel stared at me blankly. None of us spoke for a long, awkward moment.

Just when I thought my friends thought my idea was too crazy this time, Charlie said, 'I mean, it was *really* weird-looking. I guess we shouldn't rule anything out – right, Daniel?'

'Oh, come on,' he replied.

'You're supposed to be the clever one, Omar! Why would aliens steal Mrs H and disguise themselves as a hairless cat?'

I sort of knew what Daniel
meant, but I couldn't let
go of my idea that easily.
I looked up at the sky again
and then down at my feet. I noticed
something very strange then. We
were standing in a circle of grass
that was a completely different
colour to the grass
around it. I spun
round to look at the rest
of the grass and saw that
there were
four circles
just like that, making a
circle of their own on
Mrs H's front lawn.

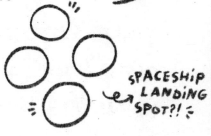

SPACESHIP
LANDING
SPOT?!

'Ermmm, guys, LOOK!' I pointed.

'That's weird,' said Charlie.

'Hmmm. What are those?' said Daniel.

They were really odd. Especially because the rest of Mrs H's garden looked like it had had somebody's very green fingers working on it, making it all pretty and neat.

'What can make weird circle patches like that?' asked Charlie.

In my head, I thought:

A SPACESHIP

And I wanted to shout out: A SPACESHIP,

GUYS! But this time, I kept it to myself,

because Daniel thought my aliens idea was too

wacky.

'I think we should get out of here,' I said,

grabbing my bike.

CHAPTER 9

We cycled slowly back towards our houses,

talking about the evidence we had seen.

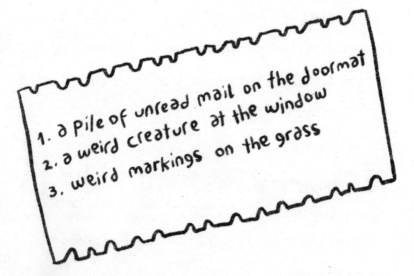

1. a pile of unread mail on the doormat
2. a weird creature at the window
3. weird markings on the grass

We decided that the first clue had to mean that she had been kidnapped and not been home for a long time. **She must still be with the captors!**

The other two clues were just weird. In my head, they were definitely alien clues. Charlie thought they could be too, but maybe he was just trying to be nice because then he said the most likely explanation was that she had been kidnapped by humans, because humans were definitely more common on Earth, so mathematically there was more chance of it being humans.

[Charlie loves m4ths.]

Daniel said there was no way it could be aliens and why were we distracting ourselves from the real kidnappers with the idea. (This is why it's good to have more than one best friend, in case one of them thinks your imagination has got out of control ...)

'Should we tell our parents?' Charlie asked.

'NOOOOOO WAY!'

said Daniel.

I thought about it. 'Hmmm. They might be able to help ... but on the other hand, they would absolutely hit the roof if they found out that I had gone outside **"the perimeter"** on my bike. YIKES.'

'The perimeter' is a very strict zone that I am allowed to ride my bike in when I'm not with Mum or Dad, or Maryam. I had broken the perimeter by *a lot* to try to save Mrs H.

'I would never, ever, ever admit to my parents how far from home we cycled,' said Daniel. 'They're coming up with more and more genius punishments for me, like they've been reading a book about it.'

'Haha, what? Like there's a book called *No Screen Time for a Week and Other Genius Punishments for Kids*.' I laughed.

'No, no,' Charlie giggled, '*209 Million Ways to Make Your Child Behave*.'

'*How to Train Your Kid and Other Animals*,' Daniel said, slapping his knee with delight.

'Seriously, though, it might be worth it, if they can help Mrs H.' I decided she was even worth losing Xbox time for a little while.

So that night, I casually walked into Mum and Dad's room, where they were reading books in bed, even though it wasn't really bedtime yet. They had chosen

Geeky science books,

obviously. But a closer look at Dad's one got me right into gear for telling them about our suspicions, because it was about the universe.

'What's up, darling?' asked Mum.

'Need batteries again?' said Dad.

Wow, how did he know that? I actually

did need batteries again, but I decided to use this time wisely and stick to the more important issue.

'No, I want to talk to you about Mrs Hutchinson ...'

'What about her? Is she back?' said Mum.

'No, that's what I want to talk about,' I said, jumping on to the bed and **wriggling** myself a space right between them.

This was great, now I could say things without having to look them in the face.

'So ... don't be mad, but ...'

'You know when you start a sentence with **"DON'T BE MAD"**, we probably will be mad,' said Mum.

'It's OK, just tell us,' said Dad. 'Maybe we will just be a teeny bit mad.'

I took a deep breath. 'OK. Well, we had to find out what happened to her, so we rode our bikes to her house and saw some stuff.'

'You r⊛de your bike outside the perimeter?

OUTSIDE it? OUT side, as in the side you promised never to go on?' said Mum, holding her head in her hands as if it would blow away if she didn't.

'Yes, but—'

'No buts!'

'And what did you see, Omar?' said Dad, who wanted to hear the rest.

The whole scene reminded me of the good

cop, bad cop thing that they talk about in films.

'We saw that her post, from many days,

was in a massive pile on the doormat, so she's

definitely missing.'

'That doesn't mean she's missing, it just means she hasn't been home for a while,' said Mum.

Dad nodded in agreement.

'Yes, but she would have said if she was going away, so it's really **SUSPICIOUS!**' I said. 'Plus, we also saw some really weird stuff ... which made me think it might be ...'

'What? What might it be?' asked Dad.

'Well, I just *think* this, and it could be true ...'

'Go on, spit it out.'

'It might be an ALIEN abduction ...'

Mum and Dad looked at each other really fast. I knew they must have made faces I couldn't see. They must have had their 'oh dear' eyebrows on.

'It's not an alien abduction, sweetie,' Mum said gently. 'Because there's no such thing as aliens ... OK?'

'Well, it depends how you define aliens,' said Dad.

I perked up and looked at him. He was

grinning .

Mum gave him a playful whack and said, 'Stop encouraging it, you!' Then she said to me, 'Mrs Hutchinson is perfectly fine, so please drop this nonsense. And as for you going outside of the perimeter, I am very disappointed.'

I let my head drop to show them I was sorry.

'I should really say that you can't go out on your bike unsupervised again,' said Mum.

'But then your fitness would suffer.' Dad finished her thoughts like he always does.

If they took away my bike rides, we wouldn't be able to continue our mission! I held my breath.

'Perhaps taking away screen time might be better,' said Dad.

No°ooooo°o.
Not my screen time!

I screamed in my head.

Out loud I said, 'You could take away

vegetables from my meals for two weeks?'

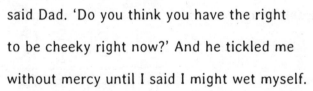

'You cheeky

little

watermelon!'

said Dad. 'Do you think you have the right

to be cheeky right now?' And he tickled me

without mercy until I said I might wet myself.

Then he said, 'Right then, Captain Cheeky

Pants. I'm proud of you for choosing to tell

us all this. But, even though you had a heroic

reason for doing it, I hope you understand

that it's a very serious thing you've done. We

put the perimeter in place to keep you safe,

because we love you. Now, you will have to

face the consequences of breaking the rules.

'Two weeks of no video games at all.'

'OK ...' I said. I knew it would be at least that anyway.

'As for the alien abduction, I'm afraid Mum's right. Aliens have not taken Mrs H. Just try to forget about it and wait and see what we hear.'

'OK ...' I said again. I climbed off Mum and Dad's bed and went to mope around in my own.

Of course they wouldn't believe us about the kidnapping, or alien abduction or whatever was happening with Mrs H. They were ADULTS without imaginations And they were boring most of the time. I wondered if my parents would have believed us if they were detectives instead of scientists. Detectives have to consider all the options, and they might even consider out-of-this-world ones, like my friends

and I were. **We were being**

GOOD DETECTIVES.

When I told Charlie and Daniel how my

parents reacted, we decided that it wasn't

worth telling any more grown ups. The school,

or the police wouldn't believe three primary

school kids more than our own parents. And

anyway, what if the school was covering

something up and telling the police would put

Mrs H in more danger when they started asking

questions!?

No. We had to get to the bottom of this

ourselves.

We decided we'd go out to investigate more

on Saturday morning.

CHAPTER 10

Friday night dinner was chicken and mushroom

pie. Mrs Rogers was over, as she sometimes is

for dinner, but she was disappointed the food

was English.

YUM!

'English food is boring,' she said, flicking off a stray flake of pastry from her purple cardigan. 'I want chilli and spice and all things nice.'

Esa giggled at the rhyming words and attempted to shovel some pie on to his fork.

'Well, Mrs Rogers, we're booking a family holiday to Pakistan. There's lots of spicy food there – maybe you should come?' Dad joked.

'Oh, I'm past my days of getting on a long flight!' said Mrs Rogers. 'But you're welcome to bring some back for me!'

Whaaaat?

We're going to Pakistan?!

It was the first I'd heard of it.

'When?' asked Maryam.

'And why?'

'Yeah, we've never been there!' I said.

'Exactly why we need to go,' said Mum.

Dad just chuckled at our confusion, before explaining that a close cousin was getting married, so we had to go for the wedding.

Mum and Dad usually daydreamed about taking us on holidays to places that other people talk about. Like Rome, to see the Colosseum, or Turkey to see the turquoise waters, or China to see the Great Wall. But Pakistan? For a wedding?!

'Nobody in my class ever talks about holidays to Pakistan,' I moaned.

'That's because nobody in your class is *from* Pakistan, silly!' said Maryam.

'I'm not from Pakistan either,' I said. 'I'm from England.'

'But your grandparents are from Pakistan,' said Dad.

'You know you're of Pakistani heritage, darling, as well as being British. It'll be nice for you to learn more about Pakistan,' Mum added.

'I'm sure it will be very interesting, Omar,' Mrs Rogers reassured me.

'But what about school?'

'We've asked your schools for some time off, because it's a big family event.'

Just then Esa let off the most stinky fart in

the universe right at
the dinner table.

Maryam, who was
sitting next to him,
suffered the most.
'Oh, Esa!!'

The hilarious
thing about Maryam
is that if she smells
something really
stinky, she starts
to gag. And that
definitely happens for
super sure if she is eating when she smells it. I
knew it was coming ...

'BLAAAAAGGGHH!'

Poor Maryam paused and tried to recover herself. She held her hand to her chest and closed her eyes.

'BLAAAAA BLAAAAA GGGHH! GGGHH!'

She stood up, put her hand over her mouth and said, 'This is what cabbages would

BLAAAAAGGGHH!

smell like BLAAAAA GGGHH!

if they were BLAAAAAGGGHH! evil.'

Mum stood up and rubbed her back, which I thought wouldn't be helping at all, so I shouted out, 'Imagine fondant fancies!' Those are

Maryam's favourite.

'BLAAAAAGGGHH!

BLAAAAAGGGHH...

Don't talk about food!' Maryam said, running out of the room.

Esa was giggling uncontrollably. Probably feeling pleased that he was able to make such a show of his bossy big sister.

Mrs Rogers looked stunned. I guess she still wasn't used to all the funny things that happen in our house.

I liked it, and for a few minutes, it made me forget about Mrs H.

CHAPTER 11

My friends came over on Saturday afternoon after I'd got back from the mosque with my family. Our first task was to make the missing posters. They were fun to make. We had a photo of Mrs Hutchinson, which Daniel had snapped from the wall at reception the day before.

It had been extremely hard, because of Mrs Crankshaw making Daniel so nervous.

'What if she has CCTV?'

Daniel had said in a whisper as we'd made our way into the classroom. 'Then she would be seeing me even if she wasn't looking my way!'

I imagined her as a fruit fly, with lots of eyes all over the place, looking at all the tables at once. **Somehow, it suited her to be a fruit fly.**

'Don't worry, teachers aren't allowed to record kids, remember?' I had reassured him.

He had his phone in his bag, which is the ONLY place phones are supposed to be if they have to come to school with a kid. Under no circumstances are kids allowed to turn them on or have them in their pocket. While the lesson was happening, I kept glancing at Daniel to see when he was going to put our plan into action.

I had never seen him sweat so much as he attempted to fish the phone out of his bag and into his pocket without Mrs Crankshaw seeing.

What happened next was the exact opposite of how we wanted it to go. It was as if Daniel was trying so hard not to be seen and heard that he accidently tripled how much he was being seen and heard.

When he was leaning under his desk to take his phone out, he managed to topple his chair all the way forward and go nose first into the floor, causing a

LOUD CRASHING NOISE

all around him.

I watched from between my fingers as Mrs
Crankshaw walked menacingly towards him.
Yikes! What if he'd had the phone in his hand
before he fell? She'd see it!

I looked at my poor friend lying in a tangled
heap on the floor. My head was spinning.
Charlie was freaking out across from me. He

was frozen in his chair, **like a deer in headlamps.** Everything went into slow motion as I desperately tried to think of what to do ...

Mrs Crankshaw's noisy pointy heels were the loudest sound in the room. She was taking long, determined strides towards Daniel. Probably plotting the most severe punishment she could, as she went.

What would make her stop? What was an even louder sound?

Yes! I had it. I looked at the four tin pencil pots sitting on our table and quick as lightning, I knocked them to the floor, making the

MOST HORRENDOUS,

metal-shattering sound on Earth.

The class winced and put their hands over

their ears. Mrs Crankshaw stopped walking

towards Daniel and spun round to walk towards

the atrocity in the opposite direction. In the

meantime, about 100 pencils and felt-tips rolled

in all directions on the floor. Some of them

must have rolled right under Mrs Crankshaw's

pointy shoe, because suddenly, she stopped

walking and **looked like she was trying**

to balance on ICE, flapping

her arms in the air for support, like some sort

of a chicken dance. The chicken dance didn't

help though – **she fell,** right on her

back, just like they do in cartoons.

The whole class gasped.

I think not so much because they felt bad for

her, but more out of fear of what she would do next.

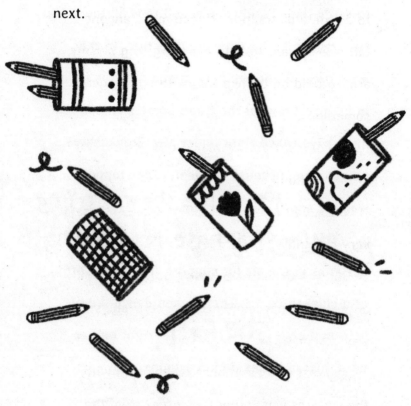

Luckily she was OK, and managed to sit up, with an embarrassed and extremely angry expression on her face.

I felt really guilty, but I had only meant to create a distraction. Not to make anyone fall over. I went to help her up, giving her my arm to hold on to, like I do with Mrs Rogers sometimes.

Of course, Daniel quickly took the chance to grab his phone.

'Miss, can I go to the toilet please?' he said, very carefully. **'My nose is bleeding.'**

But Mrs Crankshaw wasn't bothered about anything in that moment, 'Yes, yes,' she said, waving him away.

The rest was easy, because the wall with the pictures was round the corner from the reception window, so nobody saw Daniel strolling up and taking a picture.

Mrs Crankshaw made the whole class stay in

for break and sharpen every pencil in the room. My hand hurt by the end, and Ellie said she wasn't going to talk to me for a week, but at least we had our picture.

We decided to put Mrs H's photo on a Word document. We wanted to type everything out so the posters would be all professional-looking and people would take them seriously.

But it wasn't easy deciding what to put on them.

'Should we write, "Have you seen any UFOs or strange alien activity?",' suggested Charlie.

'No, that will make us look mad!' said Daniel.

'ALieNs DON'T EXIST.'

'But other people might have seen that weird alien in disguise doing things around the house,' I said.

'You mean the cat,' said Daniel. 'Maybe Mrs H shaved it because it had fleas or something.'

I decided there was no point in getting upset about Daniel not believing me. There was bound to be some more evidence soon, and then he'd come around.

We had to think about each word because we couldn't put too many words on it, otherwise the text wouldn't be big enough to read from far away. And, well, have you ever tried to say something complicated in just a few words?

After a lot of deleting and rewriting and hair pulling*, we finally decided what the poster would say.

'OK and how can people contact us? Shall we put a phone number on there, or is that too dangerous?' I asked.

'Too dangerous!' said Charlie and Daniel at the same time.

'Email address then.'

We made up an email address specially for the mission: searchformrsh@dot.com. Pretty cool, right?

---

* I just want to point out that we didn't pull *each other's* hair. We just sort of pulled our own. I've seen my dad do it before when he is typing reports on his computer. It seems to help him – like it actually gives him answers. It made me imagine that maybe Allah has built something special into the hair follicles and when you pull them a little bit, tiny invisible fairies are released which whisper the answers into your ears. It did seem to help us ... maybe.

Anyway, this is what our poster looked like:

MISSING TEACHER

HAVE YOU SEEN THIS NICE LADY?
If you have information, please email
searchformrsh@dot.com

Next, we borrowed Mum's phone and rang

Lancelot Macintosh. We had to give Mum a

gazillion reasons for being allowed to do that,

and make a trillion promises about what we would or would not say.

'Don't ask him if you can have a ride in his Ferrari. And DON'T ask him if he has a butler and DEFINITELY don't tell him aliens took his niece!' she said, before she finally asked Siri to call him and stood watching over us.

'Put him on speaker!' said Charlie.

I did.

'Hello?'

'Hello, Lancelot Macintosh!' all three of us said.

'Ah, well, if it isn't the full-name brigade! How are you!?' he chuckled.

'Good, thank you,' I said.

Mum was whispering to me to ask how he was. She's always teaching me how to be polite.

'How are you?' I asked.

'Ah, fantastic. **I'm perfectly fantastic,** thanks for asking!'

Mum looked proud.

'We were wondering ... if you knew anything about, er ... Mrs Hutchinson. She's not our teacher any more and we don't know where she is.'

'Oh dear ... right ... well. I, ahem ...' Lancelot Macintosh cleared his throat. 'I'm afraid I'm not quite sure I'm at liberty to say ... erm ... haha ...' He laughed awkwardly. 'Yes, I don't think I'm supposed to say, actually. Sorry.'

'Oh ...' I said, thinking how strangely he was behaving. **What wasn't he allowed to say?**

Then as an afterthought, and almost as if he had decided this was what he should have said to us right from the beginning, which made it sound even more secretive, he said, 'I haven't heard from that young madam in a while, anyway, ahem.'

'Oh ...'

'I'll try giving her a call and let you know if I hear anything. I'm sure she's fine, though, not to worry!'

I imagined him twiddling his long moustache as he said this, the way he always does.

I hung up the phone.

'Well, that was weird, wasn't it?!' said Daniel.

'Super weird!' I said.

'Soooo weird!' Charlie said.

'It's not weird. It sounded like he just couldn't say. And you know he doesn't *have* to tell you personal things about Mrs Hutchinson, don't you?' Mum interrupted.

I sighed and gave the phone back to her, saying, 'Yessss, Mum.' And then I saw her frowning and quickly added, 'Thanks for letting us call him.'

Mum said, 'You should start practising some words in Urdu, for our trip to Pakistan. Do you know how to say thank you in Urdu? Try to remember. You used to say it when you were little. You were so good at repeating the phrases we taught you.'

'Erm, no, I don't remember ...'

'It's Shukriya,' she said. Then she repeated it more slowly. 'Shook-ree-yah.'

'Shukriya,' I said. But as soon as she walked out of the room, we went back to wondering what Lancelot Macintosh wasn't allowed to say.

'What do you think he's not telling us?' I asked my friends.

Charlie clapped his face in his hands and gasped with shocked eyebrows. 'Do you think he knows who took her?'

'No way!' I said, immediately. 'That would make him a bad guy, and he's not a bad guy.'

'Yeah,' Daniel agreed. 'It's not that. But maybe he's not telling us about some surprise she's planning for us?'

'Yeah, he's not a bad guy. Sorry, I'm just so worried,' said Charlie.

He didn't need to tell
me that, because his
eyebrows were telling
me. Look!

'Don't worry, Charlie.
We'll keep trying,' I said.

I hoped we'd find her before we went on this
holiday.

We had to.

CHAPTER 12

After calling Lancelot Macintosh, we went out
on our bikes again. I'd had to plead with Mum
and Dad to be allowed to do this. After I had
admitted going beyond the perimeter, they
were feeling

VERY ANXIOUS

about me going out again.

I thought about promising that I wouldn't
do that again, but I knew that we needed to,
to carry on with the mission. I couldn't lie to

them. I shouldn't. I wouldn't. Even though it was really tempting.

Then I remembered that the perimeter rules were only for when I wasn't with Maryam or an adult. So even though it was super annoying and the worst change of plans in the history of the universe, I managed to let out these words in the smallest voice possible, half hoping nobody would hear them: **'What if Maryam went with us?'**

'Yes, that would be better!' said Mum.

They summoned Maryam to come out of her room, and like some mystical Rumpelstiltskin kind of creature, she emerged on the third call-out of her name, still staring at her phone as she walked down the stairs.

'What? No! No way!' she said, when Mum explained that she had to babysit my bike ride, so we wouldn't be stuck inside for the afternoon.

'Sweetie, we are giving you a big responsibility. You will be in charge. We need you to help us,' said Mum, while Dad's eyebrows were telling me he was getting ready to have to use harsher tones.

Anyway, I don't know if it was the thought of being in charge (probably, knowing Maryam), or if it was the sweet way Mum had asked, but Maryam switched attitude super fast and agreed to go.

'OK, I'll do it!'

PHEW!

The mission would go on! Even if it did mean we

had to put up with Maryam for the afternoon.

'Get into mission mode!'

I said, as all four of us cycled down the street.

'GUYS! We should think of a code name for the mission,' said Daniel excitedly.

'Like what?' said Charlie with his curious eyebrows.

'Like Operation Mrs H.'

'That's cool,' I said. 'But we should be more secrety,' I added, winking at Charlie.

Charlie grinned happily. 'Yes, more secrety for sure ... like **Operation Moon Dust**

– you know, because it could be an alien kidnapping!'

'Oh, that's awesome, I love it!' I said, beaming because Charlie was on board with my idea.

'Hmmm,' said Daniel. 'I'll go along with it, because I like moon dust.'

'You lot are such geeks,' said Maryam, rolling her eyes. 'None of you have ever even seen moon dust and there are definitely no aliens on the moon.'

'So what?!' I said. 'And anyway, yes we have.'

'**No, you haven't,**' she said.

'**Yes, we have!**' we all said together.

And we went in circles of 'no you haven't,' and 'yes we have,' the whole way to our first stop, because we were all too stubborn to give up.

The first stop was the corner shop near Mrs Hutchinson's house.

'People who come here might know something, so let's see if they will let us put a poster up,' I said, leaning my bike up against the shop window.

A bell rang as we opened the door and walked in.

'Good morning,' said the man behind the counter. But he said it exactly like it *wasn't* a good morning and he hadn't even seen who had come in. We could have been three inside-out cat-aliens and he would be none the wiser.

I walked towards him. He looked startled. I guess he was probably expecting us to wander around for ages choosing which sweets to spend our pocket money on.

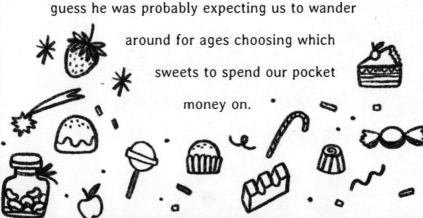

'Sorry,' I said. 'It's just that my friends and I have a question.'

I pulled out one of the missing posters from my rucksack.

Daniel pushed forward before I had the chance to say anything, excitedly pointing at the poster. 'Can we put this up?'

The corner shop man looked as if Daniel had asked him if he had seen a walking snake or something.

'No!' he said without even looking at it.

But then Charlie said, 'Please? It's for our teacher who is missing.' And he smiled his toothy smile.

The shopkeeper finally glanced at the poster and said, 'Fine. But you have to buy something.'

The three of us looked at each other, silently asking the question, 'Got any money?' None of us did, so this seemed like a big flop.

Suddenly, Maryam popped up behind us and said, 'I've got some.' She pulled out a little yellow coin purse from her jacket and to our serious surprise, she bought us each a packet of sweets. Then she took the poster from my

hand and said to the man in her bossy voice,

'**Now please put this up for us.**'

WOW.

We all made our way excitedly to the exit.

'**Thanks, Maryam!**' I said.

'Yeah, that was actually really cool of you,'

said Charlie.

And Daniel gave her a spud, which my mum

thinks is a potato, but it's not. It's a fist bump.

'Well, I do want to find out where Mrs

Hutchinson is, too,' she said. 'It's kind of

exciting, like one of those murder-mystery

books I read.'

Daniel was walking backwards through the shop door, because he had spun round for the spud, and as he stepped out on to the street, he fell right on to Ellie from our class.

Ellie squealed as if she had just been covered in zombie snot.

'ARGH! Get off me!'

Sarah was with her. 'What are you all doing here anyway?' she said, still on her scooter.

'None of your business!' said Daniel, picking himself up and helping Ellie off the floor.

'We're just buying sweets,' I said, holding up my packet.

Charlie and Daniel both flashed their packets too, with cheeky grins.

'But this isn't YOUR local shop—' said Ellie.

'Whatever,' Daniel interrupted. '**Byeeee!**'

We grabbed our bikes and sped off before

they got any nosier.

'I think she heard what Maryam said about

finding out where Mrs H is,' said Daniel.

'She must have. We were talking

really loudly,' said Charlie.

Hmmm, I thought. We

didn't want people at school

knowing what we were up to,

because if they told the teachers,

they'd either think we were silly, just

like my parents did, or if they were

really in on her disappearance, then

we'd be in danger. I had no idea it

was also their local shop. I hoped the

grumpy shopkeeper would wait

until they left to put our poster up.

'Let's put the rest of them up on lampposts and trees around the area.' I said.

We had brought blue tack and sticky tape with us. It was quite fun – Operation Moon Dust! It finally felt like we were doing something to help that could actually work. Someone had to know something, and they would email us soon. I was sure.

We tried to cover lots of roads in the area. When we were making our way

to the third road, we heard a scream behind us.
It was Ellie and Sarah. Ellie had fallen off her
scooter again.

'Have they been following us?!' I said,

PANICKING.

'They're so nosey!' said Charlie.

We rode up to them quickly.

Sarah was picking an embarrassed Ellie up
from the floor for a second time.

'It's not my fault I can't balance, I'm still
recovering from you!' she said, pointing at
Daniel.

'Have you been following us?' I asked.

'No! We're just going home,' said Sarah.

'Yeah, you guys don't own the roads, do
you?' said Ellie, with a hand on her hip.

'Why are you acting so strangely? What exactly are you up to?' said Sarah.

I tried to read her eyebrows, but I couldn't. Did she already know? Had they seen the posters? Or were they question-mark eyebrows? She wouldn't keep them still. She was moving her eyebrows up and down and then one up and one down. It was driving me crazy!

Ellie was staring at us, waiting for an answer, which she wasn't going to get.

'Stop being so nosey and get on with your own business,'

said Maryam.

'Is your knee OK, Ellie?' asked Charlie, blushing. 'Did you hurt yourself when you fell down?'

Charlie is always super nice to everyone. It's why we became best friends in the first place, but I suddenly realised we had to get him away before he spilled the beans. If Ellie started sniffing about her sore knee, he would definitely tell her whatever she asked!

'Come on, guys, let's go!' I said and we

pedalled home again. It was time to wrap up

Operation Moon Dust for the day.

CHAPTER 13

For a couple of weeks, we didn't really know

what else we could do for Operation Moon

Dust. I had filled Mrs Rogers in, and she said

we had done *great work*, but

that now we just had to wait and see what

happened. I didn't tell her about the alien

clues, though, just about our posters and

Daniel's close encounter with getting caught

with his phone in his hand in class.

Until somebody reached out to us with

another clue, we had no choice but to carry on

our boring lessons with

MrS CrANky For Sure.

That was the new name everyone in the class

was using for her. Even Sarah, who had been

compared to an angel by more than one of the

teachers at school, had started

calling her by her new name

in the playground (away

from Mrs C's pointy ears).

POINTY EAR

I tried to butter up Mrs

Crankshaw so she'd be nicer to

us all, by giving her a scone that Mrs Rogers

had made. Mrs Rogers had winked at me when

she brought them over, saying, 'These scones

have been known to turn hearts. Try offering

one to your new teacher. You never know, she

might be transformed.'

'Wow, thank you!' I had said hopefully.

Esa said, 'Shukriya,' because he was practising his Urdu words. Of course, Mum was super impressed with that.

But Mrs Crankshaw was not impressed at *all* with the scone. She said, 'You know you shouldn't bring people food, because you don't know what food allergies they might have!'

'Oh ... sorry,' I said, with a lump in my throat.

Charlie had to give me a hug to make me feel better after that. And my stomach wouldn't stop feeling weird all through literacy. I felt like I was going to throw up my morning porridge. I have done that before, and it's not very pretty. Porridge isn't the prettiest food in the first place and after having been in a stomach, it doesn't get any better looking!

Remembering the time I vomited porridge
made me feel even worse, so I stood up
quickly and asked if I could go to the toilet. I

must have looked kind of green, because Mrs Crankshaw said 'yes' immediately, and she looked scared when she said it.

When I left the classroom, I felt better straight away. As if it was the toxic rays from Mrs C in there that were making me sick. Then a voice popped into my head out of nowhere. And it sounded a lot like Maryam.

'Somebody knows ...'

it said.

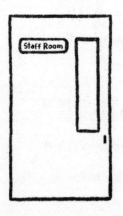

And just like that, my feet turned me towards the staffroom, with my heart thumping.

There were no teachers going in and out of the staffroom. The corridor was abandoned. But

I could hear voices inside. I looked around quickly to make sure no one was coming and put my ear to the door. I had to work hard to make out the words:

'More marking! I wish *mumble* *mumble* long break instead!' said one voice.

'*mumble* *mumble* Hazel?' replied a second voice.

My ears perked up even more because Hazel is Mrs Hutchinson's name!

'Ha! Not like she had a choice *mumble* *mumble* She was throwing up left, right and *mumble* *mumble* take her in for loads of tests.'

'Just imagine, *mumble* *mumble* living inside you *mumble* *mumble* all that chaos!'

Something living inside her?

'Haha, *mumble* *mumble*
I guess she'll be that way until it comes out
mumble *mumble*'

'Will you visit *mumble* *mumble*?'

'Gosh no, I'm not *mumble* *mumble*
person, they're so weird-looking at *mumble*
mumble I prefer when they're more like
real humans *mumble**mumble*, haha.'

What I was hearing seemed to confirm
everything I had seen and imagined! I quickly
walked away with my head in my hands, trying
to make sense of it all.

Until it comes out? Something inside her?
Making her throw up? Weird looking? More like
real humans? They took her for tests?

It all fell into place. Of course!

It HAD TO BE aliens!

But it was worse than we had thought: Mrs Hutchinson had swallowed an alien, so the aliens had taken her away to poke at her until it came out! I couldn't believe our teachers were secretly in league with a bunch of aliens – or maybe even *were* aliens themselves!

It was just AWFUL.

When I got back into the classroom, I didn't care about getting told off by Mrs Crankshaw any more, I couldn't do any work and just stared at my books until break time when I could talk to my friends properly. Mrs Hutchinson had been taken by aliens! I knew it sounded out of this world, but I was absolutely convinced.

We found a quiet spot and I spilled everything I'd heard. Charlie was in shock and just opened and closed his mouth loads of times. Daniel said, **'But aliens don't exist...?'**

It was the same sentence he had been saying ever since we saw the clues at Mrs Hutchinson's, but now he said it as a question, as if he wasn't sure what to believe any more.

'Think about it. Mrs Hutchinson herself said that aliens are out there and they might be watching us!' I said.

'Yeah, and scientists wouldn't be bothering to look for aliens in outer space if they didn't think they existed,' added Charlie, recovering from his fish impression.

'Come to think of it, I did see her rubbing her tummy one day ...' said Daniel. 'But how could she have swallowed an alien? Like *why* would she?'

'Maybe they're so tiny you can't even see them, and they had come to spy on her for teaching us that alien lesson,' I said.

'So, she ate it by accident?' said Charlie.

'Yes, *or* she ate it on purpose, to save us, because the aliens were threatening to hurt her class?' I said.

'Wow, she's so brave!' said Charlie.

'But this is CRAZY!' said Daniel, unable to accept it just yet. 'There has to be another explanation.'

'Sometimes, Daniel, the craziest explanations are the correct ones! Dad told me that happens a lot in science.'

'So, what are we going to do now?' said Charlie.

We decided it was best to try to speak to some space scientists and do some research on Google on extra-terrestrial visitors to Earth to start with.

Operation Moon Dust really was going to outer space!

CHAPTER 14

Over the next few days, we spent lunchtimes

in the school library, researching everything

we could about aliens, mostly for Daniel, who

still wasn't convinced that Mrs Hutchinson had

been sucked up into space by them. And man

did we find some weird stuff that absolutely

confirmed that aliens were out there and were

even found on Earth. Well, the online articles

didn't *actually* call them aliens, they called

them 'organisms' but they said

that these weird tiny squiggly things proved

there was life on other planets. One writer

said the organisms look like dragons, but they

obviously have no idea what dragons look like.

They should see my H_2O –

that's what

a dragon

Looks Like!

There was a whole universe of stuff to read on Google. We didn't understand a lot of the words and I wished we could ask my parents to explain them. They'd know about things like what on earth the 'Copernican principle' is, but then they'd know we were still convinced that aliens had abducted our teacher.

Mrs Hutchinson always said that when we do research, we should look at 'sources we can trust', which basically means, if it is written by a famous organisation that is known for being right about things, we can usually believe them. Whereas if it's a blog written by people like Maryam and her friends, we should be careful.

WELL! We found a BBC article by a Nasa CHIEF scientist, saying that they were definitely about to find life on other planets in the coming years. That's two sources we could trust.

'Do you see, Daniel?' said Charlie excitedly. 'Do you beliiiieeeeeeeve?' and he spun Daniel's whirly chair round to look him in the eyes for extra dramatic effect.

Just then, Ellie and Sarah walked into the library, with extra nosey expressions painted all over their faces.

'Does he believe what?' pressed Ellie.

They tried to look at our computer screen, but I quickly closed the window AND stood in front of it, just in case.

Charlie frantically gathered the few books on space that we had found on the shelves and sat on them.

We wouldn't share our secret, no matter how much they bugged us to, so they went to sit down and pretended to read some books on history. Sarah and Ellie hated history lessons,

So we KNEW they were just spying.

We had to pack it up that day, but we felt super proud of ourselves for looking into the idea properly, and even being able to convince Daniel (sort of). The next time we were able to get into the library, we found an email contact for NASA and sent them all the details from our searchformrsh@dot.com address. Perhaps they would send out a special search mission in space for her? After all, it was their job, wasn't it?

We kept a close eye on our inbox, but they didn't reply to us, no matter how much we checked.

While we waited for something to happen, we tried to get on with our lives as if everything was normal. Even though Maryam had been nice about helping us put the missing posters up, we didn't share our alien abduction idea with her, because she would

DEFiNiTELY
LAUGH AT US

and tell all her friends, who would also join in with the laughing. I had to keep it all to myself at home, which was HARD.

Maybe because of all the keeping it to myself inside my head, I saw aliens everywhere. Instead of seeing regular old fruit flies, I would see tiny flying aliens, and imagine them growing into something much bigger and slimier when they landed on a surface. And instead of seeing Esa's green snot as regular green snot, I would see it as alien slime.

One day, when we were in a shopping centre and I was desperate for a wee, I could have sworn I saw an alien peek his head out of one of the toilets, to see if anyone was around.

CHAPTER 15

At home, things were quite busy, as Mum and
Dad prepared for our trip to Pakistan.

My friends were

super jealous

about me being allowed to take time off school
and go on holiday, while they had to have
boring lessons with Mrs CrankyForSure.

'We will probably literally die of boredom
without you, Omar,' said Charlie. 'Can you

clone yourself and leave one of you here?'

'Yeah, do that! You're good at science, you can figure it out,' Daniel added.

I giggled, imagining myself as a clone.

Would my clone have all of my memories?

Would he be good at science too?

'What's Pakistan like, anyway?' Charlie asked.

'I have **NO CLUE**. The only thing I've heard was from my cousin who said the pizza is yuck' I said.

I soon found out another thing about the food in Pakistan because one Tuesday, Dad came home with three bags full of chocolate.

WHAAAAAT?

Three bags of my favourite food?

Obviously, Esa, Maryam and I pounced on him right away, attempting to wrestle him to the ground to rob him of all the bags.

Dad laughed and then roared and said, 'Hulk angry,' pretending to be angry, which we knew he wasn't.

Then he said, 'Actually ... Hulk hungry!
What's for dinner, oh mother
of mischievous children?'

Mum laughed and said that we were *his*
children when we were mischievous, and we
were only hers when we were
little angels like she is.

'I want chocolate for
dinner,' said Esa.

'Well, these chocolates are
for all the different families we will
visit in Pakistan. The chocolate they get out
there is nowhere as good as this
stuff,' said Dad.

'Pleeeeease ... I will say
shukriya?' said Esa, making
his puppy eyes.

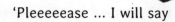

150

Everyone laughed at his suggestion. Usually Esa would laugh too, but for some reason he stood still, thinking. Then he asked very carefully, 'Mum? How do you laugh in Urdu?'

That was the best thing Esa had said in a while.

In the end, Dad allowed us to have some of the chocolate if we could prove he had a brain. He likes to play games with us like that.

'You do have one, obviously!' said Maryam. 'Otherwise how could you be a scientist?'

'That's not proof. Mrs Rogers isn't a scientist, does that mean she doesn't have a brain?' teased Dad.

'You have one because you're talking and walking and things!' I said.

'Good!' said Dad, winking my way. 'I'd definitely need a brain for that.'

'OK, you have one because you're human and all humans have brains. We know that because scientists have looked at lots of human bodies,' said Maryam, trying harder.

'Excellent!' said Dad, and he rewarded us with a bar each.

Maryam doesn't like science like the rest of our family. She's always grumpy on

Science Sundays,

which is when we do fun science experiments in the kitchen, and one day recently when Mum was tutoring Maryam on science, she seemed super bored, and then she suddenly burst out crying. It was a painful crying, like something really, really bad had happened.

'Maryam, what is it?' asked Mum, jumping to put her arms around her. 'Has something happened in school? Tell me?'

Maryam had continued to cry, like she was being tortured.

'Maryam, sweetie, please tell me. I can't help you if you don't tell me,' pleaded Mum.

'YOU'RE TRYING TO MAKE ME GOOD AT SCIENCE!'

Mum looked shocked.

'I thought that was nice of me,' she said.

'Pardon me, young lady, I thought I was helping you!'

Mum tried to be cross when saying this, but she found Maryam's reason for crying very, very funny and she couldn't hold it in any more – she burst out laughing, which made Maryam cry even more.

Mum hugged her and told her that she was already good at science, but if she loved other subjects more, the way she loved art, she could be something creative instead of being a scientist.

It seemed like that made Maryam feel a whole let better.

CHAPTER 16

With a one-week countdown to our trip, I started to get REALLY excited about having a break from Mrs Crankshaw. Why? Because she had banned smiling in class! We didn't suspect her of being a super-villain for no reason.

It had happened on a day when we were learning about South America. Obviously, Mrs Crankshaw had made it boring with her super boring-making powers. She had asked us to

read about it from a textbook and 'make notes'.
Daniel finds that kind of thing impossible, so
instead of getting on with it, he busied himself
by leaning on the two back legs of his chair
and smiling over at Charlie and me.

We had a whole **'smile conversation'.**

'Sheesh, this is boring,' smiled Daniel.

'Super definitely,' I smiled back.

'Can't wait till lunchtime,' smiled Charlie.

'Can't wait till the holidays,' smiled Daniel.

But that was his last smile for a bit, because
just then there was a big

as the two back legs of Daniel's chair gave in, and he went tumbling into the book display behind him. What was it with Daniel always falling off his chair??

'Right!!!' screamed Mrs Crankshaw.

'I've been watching you, Daniel Green. All of this happened because of your silly smiling. There will be no more silly smiling. Do you hear that, everyone? There will be no more smiling in this class, ever.'

And she stamped her pointy heel on the ground like she was an army general and wrote

'NO SMILING'

on the board.

We were miserable that lunchtime. Why did
Mrs CrankyForSure have to be so mean?

We tried to think of the reasons:

'Maybe she was bitten by a mysterious bug
from Mars that makes people grumpy for the
rest of their days,' I said.

'Maybe she has Grumpy Nut
Cornflakes for breakfast every
morning,' said Charlie.

'Maybe she farts toxic fumes that
make her angry and mean when she
accidently
breathes
them in,' said Daniel.

We had a good giggle at
that, which cheered us up a
little and we decided to spend

some of lunchtime in the school library so we could check the inbox for an email from NASA. Operation Moon Dust was always on our mind.

I logged in, without much hope, because the last 38 times I had done this, there was no email. But as the page loaded, our eyes fell on an email with the subject line:

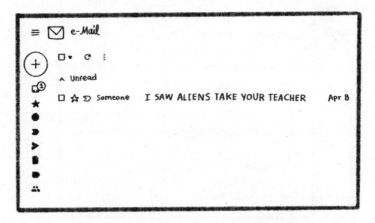

I nearly fell off my chair, and Daniel gave Charlie an excited whack on the back which was way too hard and sent him off on a spluttering coughing fit.

When we all recovered enough, I said, 'Let's open it ...'

It read:

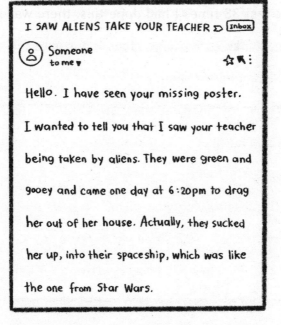

I SAW ALIENS TAKE YOUR TEACHER ➤ Inbox

Someone
to me ▾   ☆ ⬏ ⋮

Hello. I have seen your missing poster.

I wanted to tell you that I saw your teacher being taken by aliens. They were green and gooey and came one day at 6:20pm to drag her out of her house. Actually, they sucked her up, into their spaceship, which was like the one from Star Wars.

We were utterly gobsmacked. Even Daniel didn't say a word for a long time.

'Poor Mrs Hutchinson,' I said eventually.

'I can't believe it,' said Charlie with sad eyebrows.

'I will kill those aliens! **And make them eat avocadoes!'** said Daniel, who thinks eating avocadoes is the worst punishment imaginable.

'How can they eat them after they're dead?' asked Charlie.

'Oh, they will!'

'I guess this only confirms what we already know,' I said. 'And since we haven't got a rocket, we will have to keep waiting on help from the real astronauts. They have to help! Maybe they are, secretly, already?'

Still, the pictures that email had put in our heads were terrible. It made everything more real. And now we had a description of the aliens. Green and gooey. Mrs H must have been terrified. I imagined what her hair looked like when she was scared. Probably the way they show it in cartoons when someone gets an electric shock. All the curls rigid and standing on end.

CHAPTER 17

We spent the whole rest of the week not
smiling in class. Even during the last lesson on
Friday, which meant a weekend was beginning
and everyone would normally be *Super*
happy. During that lesson, though,
it sort of looked like Mrs Crankshaw was
'smiling'. Her mouth was turning up at the
corners ever so slightly, but as if it hurt to do
it. I guessed that she was happy because she
had managed to invent the most miserably
boring lesson possible.

Charlie noticed it first and nudged me as we tried to keep our eyes open, 'Hey ... is Mrs CrankyForSure *smiling*?'

'No *way* ...' I whispered.

'Shall we ask her if the smile ban has been lifted?'

That made me laugh. And as I had just taken a sip from my water bottle, it made it come out of my nose. **OUCH that kills!**

Never ever laugh with a drink in your mouth.

If I was an alien who had come to Earth for the first time, and I came to Mrs Crankshaw's class, I would think that all teachers were grumpy and boring. But they're not. I know that because of Mrs Hutchinson. She really, really is

the best.

We flew out to Pakistan the next day, from Heathrow Airport.

Mrs Rogers waved us off from her front garden with a tear in her eye.

'We'll be back before you know it, Mrs Rogers,' said Dad.

'Oh, I disagree. I'm afraid I'll miss you all too much!'

We gave her hugs and thanked her for the treats she had baked for us to have on the way.

'I'll bring you back something Pakistani,' I said.

'You're the only Pakistani thing I need,' she joked.

I smiled at the thought of her finding the

little notes I had left around her house when she fell asleep on the sofa the evening before we were leaving.

In her teapot: 'I miss you too, Mrs Rogers.'

Halfway through the book she's reading:

'Here's a joke for you: Why don't aliens eat clowns? Because they taste funny!'

Behind a sofa cushion:

'Will you finally tell me your big secret from when you were younger, when I get back?'

Inside her special garden shoes:

'Are you surviving without Pakistani food?'

On the plane, we did what we always do.

Maryam and I fought for the **window seat** and Esa and I fought to sit next to

Dad. We each had our own rucksack full of

things to keep us busy, and as a special travel

treat, **we had sweets!**

Mum made us pack books to read, and

puzzles to do, because she didn't want us to

continuously watch the films on the in-flight

entertainment for the whole eight-hour flight.

Even with all the stuff to do, the flight was

LOOOOONG.

I felt odd being stuck in one seat for eight

hours, with nowhere to go except a smelly

toilet that made a scary noise when you flushed

it. I looked out of the window and wondered

how much further up I would have to

go to get to space. I imagined my

dragon H_2O picking me up from

the wing of the plane and

flying us both upwards,

Like a rocket. ⌣

Then I thought about the second message we had received from the same person to our MrsH email address. I had picked it up just before we'd had to rush to the car that morning, so I hadn't had a chance to tell Daniel or Charlie yet. It said:

I saw her swallow an alien by the way. And I know where she is.

Who was this person? How did they know so much? Was it her neighbour? Or the funny man at the corner shop?

We eventually got through the flight and finally started seeing Pakistan from way up high, before we made a smooth landing at Lahore International Airport. That's the capital city in Pakistan.

My uncle came to collect us from the

airport. He isn't *really* my *uncle* uncle, he's my dad's older cousin, but in Pakistan we knew to call all the adults in the family 'uncle' and 'aunty', and all the kids 'cousin'. He had a moustache like Lancelot Macintosh's, and no hair, which made me giggle, because he looked like an egg with a moustache.

I kept that to myself, because I knew Mum would absolutely *not* be proud of me for making fun of the way someone looks. Well, it wasn't making fun if I only thought it inside my head and didn't put it into anyone else's head.

On the drive to my uncle's house, I decided

I already loved Pakistan.

It was different to any place I had ever seen.

The cars were all beeping and bouncing into

whichever lanes they wanted, and every so

often, there was a random donkey pulling a

cart in the same lane as all the cars, and three-

wheeled vehicles, called rickshaws, which

looked like they were part of a circus act! It

was noisy and dirty, but it was

AMAAAAAAZiNG!

CHAPTER 18

 The houses were big in Pakistan. Well, at least my uncle's was, and all the others I saw from the car. There were maids at his house too, who cleared up after us and served us

yummy food,

which was better than my mum's Pakistani cooking.

I asked Mum if everyone in Pakistan had a maid, or if my uncle was a billionaire like the queen or something. She told me that it was quite common and laughed at the idea our family was **$UP£R R1CH.**

Can you imagine having a maid at home? I couldn't believe it!

I had twin cousins, called Amber and Ambreen, who always wore matching shalwar kameez, which is the traditional Pakistani outfit of a tunic over soft trousers.

AMBER

AMBREEN

It made it really hard to tell them apart, which they enjoyed very much.

'You talk so fast,' they kept saying, in their Pakistani accent. And they would giggle for ages when Maryam and I got into a squabble and called each other names like

FR🐸G FACE

and

RHIN🦏 NOSE.

My aunty didn't say much, but she always made a point to tell her daughters to stop giggling.

Early in the mornings, **I would hear the strangest calls.**

It sounded like a man's voice, but I couldn't make out what he was saying. It wasn't the call to prayer, which is called **the adhan,** because I knew exactly what that sounded like.

I used to hear it lots when we went on holiday to Turkey once, and I was hearing it in Lahore too, coming from the mosques. But I needed to know what this other morning call was so, one day, the minute I heard it, I ran to the balcony and saw a man pulling a cart full of fresh vegetables, calling out:

'Aalooooo Layyyyllo,

Pyqaaqaz Layyyyllo,

gaaajar Layyyyyyyyllo!'

I asked Amber and Ambreen what he was calling out, although I could tell it was something about the vegetables.

'He's saying get potatoes, get onions, get carrots!' They both giggled almost at the same time, finding it hilarious that I didn't understand Urdu.

So, I said, 'Shukriya,' for fun. Because it was about the only word I could remember at the time.

After a few days, we went to meet Yusuf, the man who was getting married; the reason I was missing school and had come all the way to a place I had never been to before. He was my mum's aunty's son. **I got very confused** about whether that meant I should call him a cousin, even though he wasn't a kid. But Mum said he could just be 'Uncle' too! Apparently, Mum used to go on holiday to Pakistan a lot before she got busy being an IMPORTANT SCIENTIST and had us kids, so she had been quite close with this part of the family and it was out of the question for her not to be here to share the joy. Although, I think Mum was just excited to have an excuse to show us the country her parents were from. (In case you're wondering, my grandparents had decided not to come on this trip. My nani said we were all representing them at the wedding, so had to be on our best behaviour.)

Uncle Yusuf was really nice, so I was glad

we had come. 'This is the groom – Yusuf,' Mum said proudly.

'He's not a broom!'

said Esa.

Yusuf laughed and pulled out all sorts of presents for us. He was a giant man, even taller than Dad, but he had a super gentle voice. Esa looked tiny in front of him, and when Yusuf picked him up, he did it as carefully as if he was made of **eggshells.**

'What have they been feeding you at Aunty and Uncle's?' he laughed as he popped Esa on his shoulder. 'Shrinking powder? This little man looks about the same size as my head!'

After meeting him, I was looking forward to going to his big wedding. I wanted to see what the bride was like.

I hoped she'd be kind, like him.

CHAPTER 19

One evening, when were all sitting around at my uncle and aunty's house, my aunty announced that the special wedding outfits she had been busy having made for us had finally arrived.

They were wrapped up in colourful cotton sheets, which she excitedly opened up, one by one.

Ouch, they looked really uncomfortable, with rock hard collars. They were the same type of thing that my cousins wear every day, except extra fancy.

Maryam liked hers a lot, probably because it looked like a princess dress, with sparkly patterns and beads. She even got some gold shoes to go with it.

GOLD! SUPER YUCK!

Of course, I was forced to try mine on, so I took it to the twins' room, which was closest. I put it on the bed and wasted some time before having to put it on by **snooping around a bit.** They were laughing at me for not knowing how to speak Urdu, maybe I would find something to tease them about ...

There wasn't much around. Just some books

and board games. But just when I was about to give up on finding anything interesting, my foot tapped something hard. I looked down.

FLYING FISH EGGS!

It was a telescope! What were Amber and Ambreen doing with a telescope?

I threw my wedding outfit on in a millisecond (it didn't actually look too bad) so I could go and ask them about it.

'To look into outer space, of course,' said Amber. **WOW!**

Who knew they would be so cool! *I liked them ten times* more,* right on the spot.

Maryam and I begged them to let us have a go.

'Pleeeease show us how to look at the planets!' I said, obviously thinking of Mrs H. It was a long shot, but maybe I would see an alien spaceship or something. Maybe there would be more clues that would help us.

It turned out, Amber and Ambreen knew lots about space. They were proper space geeks.

They let us take turns to look through it, excitedly telling us what to look for.

'I've been on another planet,' said Esa.

'No, you haven't, Esa,' I told him.

'Yes, I did go!' Esa protested.

'No,' said Maryam. 'Don't fib.'

'Yes, Dad said "he's on another planet," when I wasn't listening. So, I did!'

Amber and Ambreen giggled and pulled Esa's cheek.

'He is sooooo cute,' they said.

It was my turn to look. I took hold of the telescope carefully.

'Have you ever seen a spaceship or an alien?' I asked, trying to be casual.

Maryam said, 'Of course they haven't, pineapple prickles! Because those don't exist.'

'Actually, they might,'

said Amber.

'They probably do,' said Ambreen.

Maryam rolled her eyes.

'Wow ... did you see something?' I asked, wide eyed.

'Yes, we see strange things all the time, but we don't know what they are.'

'Do you think they ever come down to Earth?' I paused '... and ... er ... take stuff?'

At that, Maryam exploded with laughter and let herself fall to the floor to roll around holding her belly, to show just how funny it was.

'OMAR! You think they took Mrs Hutchinson don't you?' she teased.

'No!' I lied. 'Of course not!'

But Maryam fanned the air, pretending she couldn't even breathe with how hilarious it was, and then walked out of the room.

'Who's Mrs Hutchinson?' asked Amber.

'Never mind ...' I whispered, with a lump in my throat. And I quickly walked away before they noticed how sad I was.

CHAPTER 20

I was making fun of James or Justin, or

Maliha. My dad was standing at the door

I liked Yusuf so much that I didn't mind putting

on the uncomfortable fancy wedding clothes

when it was time. When I looked in the mirror,

I looked like a different kid!

Like my own Pakistani twin.

Amber and Ambreen were wearing matching

outfits. Maryam had put on her princess clothes

and looked very pleased with herself. She was

trying to take selfies on her phone, to show her friends.

The house was busy with people running around looking for their shoes or putting on lipstick. My dad was standing at the door shouting about getting into the car already, which my uncle found hilarious.

'Don't worry, everybody will be late. **Nobody goes On time'.** he said, chilling out on the sofa.

'What? Uncle? Are you even dressed?' asked Dad.

'No, no, the ladies will take too long. I will get dressed in a minute,' he chuckled.

This was very difficult for Dad, who thinks it's the end of the world to be late to anything. So, being told he had to be late on purpose was pretty much the same as being told he had to eat through his nose! He checked his watch longingly and sat down uncomfortably in his outfit.

We finally piled into the car. When we arrived, we saw Uncle was totally right: EVERYONE was late. Now, I've been to Pakistani weddings in London before, but this was something different. It was crazy!

Good crazy, <u>not</u> WILD CRAZY.

It was outdoors, but in a BIG MARQUEE, which is just a fancy word for a tent that is the size of a big house. It was decorated with lights – so many of them on the inside and outside! There were hundreds and hundreds of people there. In a way, it was like a game, because there were 'sides'. We were on the groom's side, which meant we had to make a *Grand Entrance* with him.

You're not going to believe this, but Yusuf made his entrance on a horse. A dressed-up horse! And the horse looked just big enough to take his weight, but only just. And there were other horses that were dancing. A few men were playing the biggest drums I have ever seen, which they hung around their necks. The sound was **HUGE.**

And it was a good tune. It made me want to

dance walk, instead of normal walk my way into the marquee.

The bride's side were already inside, and they threw lots of flower petals on us as we walked in. Together with the fancy clothes

everyone was wearing, *it was a*

BiG EXPLOSiON of CoLouRS.

Esa was loving it and Maryam was trying to love it, but she was also busy complaining about how **itchy** her princess dress turned out to be. Amber and Ambreen looked like they weren't seeing anything special, probably because they see these kinds of big Pakistani weddings all the time.

Then the bride came in. Maryam's princess clothes were nothing compared to hers. She was wearing a dark red dress that was so long, she couldn't actually walk unless someone was lifting it for her a bit.

It looked **HEAVY** too, with MILLIONS of GEMS and BEADS.

Yusuf and his bride, Aisha, sat together and then a man in a hat and a beard came to talk to them.

'That's the imam,' Mum explained. **'He's going to marry them now.'**

A lot of people were still chatting away, which I thought was crazy. 'They're missing it!' I said.

It was over in just a couple of minutes. He just asked them to say some words and sign a paper and that was it! Yusuf was married to Aisha, **and half the people missed it!**

When the food came, I couldn't believe how much there was. There were so many things to eat, I couldn't even try them all. Most of it was too full of chilli for me, anyway – which is weird because I thought **I LOVED** spicy food.

And at the end, when it was time for the bride and groom to go, everyone cried lots and lots like something bad had happened. That was super weird. It was a wedding and weddings are supposed to be happy, right?

'Why are they crying?'

I asked Maryam.

'Probably because their clothes are too uncomfortable,' she replied, tugging her itchy *BLINK* dress away from her skin and walking painfully in her golden heels.

'It's sort of like a tradition,' explained Dad. 'It's the girl's side that is crying, because they are sad that she's leaving their family.'

'But she's not, is she? She'll be back and still see them?' I asked.

'Of course,' said Dad.

Traditions were funny things, sometimes, I guessed.

I imagined they saw Yusuf as a giant alien in disguise that was abducting her and taking her to outer space for ever on his dancing horse, which seemed funny for a minute until I remembered that that's exactly what could have happened to Mrs H.

I gulped.

CHAPTER 21

Now that the wedding events were over, we had more free time. I looked through the telescope every chance I could get. I was glued to it one evening when we were supposed to be going out to a restaurant for dinner. Everyone had been looking for me around the big house, and I didn't hear them calling, so Maryam was super cross when she had to come and find me.

'There you are! You're so **obsessed** with that thing,' she said.

'Hurry up.'

Oh man, just when I was trying to get a flying object back into focus! I had to drop it and run.

On the way to the restaurant it was really windy. But it wasn't just a regular wind – it was blowing dirt around everywhere, so we couldn't open the car windows. Apparently, that kind of wind happens all the time in Lahore.

When we got to the restaurant car park it was filled with fancy cars. A man came to knock on the windows of the car, putting his hand out. His clothes were dirty and torn and he didn't have any shoes on. **My uncle tried to shoo him away.**

'Mum, what's that man saying?' I asked.

Oh, Sweetie, he's a poor man. He's asking for money.'

Dad pulled out a couple of notes of Pakistani currency and handed them to him. He started saying lots of things in Urdu.

'Now what's he saying?' I asked.

'He's praying for goodness and blessings for Dad,' said Mum.

I felt so sad for the poor old man. He didn't have any money, and all the people in the fancy cars obviously had lots.

Just then, lots more poor people started coming up to Dad, making it impossible for him to get out of the car. My uncle shooed them away, muttering angry Urdu words.

I wish I had Lots of my own money to give them.

'Can we invite them to dinner?' I asked as we were walking into the restaurant.

'Of course we can't, gerbil brains,' said Maryam.

I paused and turned around just to have one more look at them. But when I did, I almost fell to the floor because of what I saw ...

It was Mrs Hutchinson!!!

She was getting into a Black Toyota and her

belly was # BIG.

I couldn't believe it. I blinked a few times, just to make sure. **It WAS her.** Every bit of curly hair and smile and A BIG BELLY! We had been looking for her for ages, and suddenly she was right before my eyes. My legs threatened not to hold me up any more, but fast as I could I rushed in and found my parents. I told them I needed to speak to my friends right away. I was a **TOTAL** mess.

'Just a minute. What is going on?' said Dad.

'Mrs Hutchinson's on Earth, I mean she's come back down to Earth, she's here, I just saw her and her tummy is big, like

THE ALIEN IS STILL IN THERE,

She must have escaped. She MUST have swallowed an alien. What is she doing HERE? Maybe she landed in the complete wrong country. Maybe she was with the FBI. Maybe she IS FBI.

Argggghhghhghgh,'

I spluttered all in one go.

'Wow,' said Mum.

My uncle and aunty were looking at me as if they had in that moment decided that all British kids were completely **bonkers.**

They were looking from me to Mum and Dad and nodding their heads as if in agreement with their own thoughts.

'Right, take a seat, son,' said Dad and he poured me a glass of water. 'Tell me what you're talking about, calmly.'

Hmmm, could I? I knew it was unbelievable to them. I felt like I'd already said too much, so I stayed quiet.

'Him and his weird friends think Mrs Hutchinson was abducted by aliens,' teased Maryam.

SHE MADE iT SOUND SO STUPiD.

'Are you still on that?' asked Mum.

'Sort of,' I said, even though I 100 per cent was.

'Let's calm down and have some food, darling. You're just hungry and tired,' said

Mum, and she gave me a cuddle.

'Well, she could have swallowed an alien ...' said Dad, causing all the heads to spin around to glare at him.

'Kidding!' he said, having a good chuckle.

'Am I not allowed to have an imagination like my boy's?'

And just like that, everyone settled down and took their plates around the fabulous buffet, collecting all sorts of fancy foods. But I had lost my appetite.

CHAPTER 22

I hated Maryam for making my idea sound stupid in front of Mum and Dad, but she was the only one I could talk to about it all.

I told her that **I HADN'T imagined seeing Mrs Hutchinson.**

'When I imagine things, I know I'm imagining them, Maryam. I know the difference between seeing something and imagining it ...'

'I get that,' said Maryam.

PHEW! I must have caught the good Maryam. She's a teenager so she changes from being that and evil Maryam in minutes.

'Thanks for believing me ...'

'So, you saw her? Who was she with?'

'I don't know. I just saw her getting into a car.'

'OK. But you do know that the outer space thing is completely crazy, right?'

'We have lots of proof,' I tried.

'You *think* you do.'

'Do you think we can go back to that restaurant and look for her again?'

'Probably not. Anyway, it's not as if she would eat there every night. But we can look out for her every time we go out.'

'OK.' I said. At least that was something. But we needed all the help we could get, so I lifted my hands up to make a dua, and asked Allah to help. That had helped in the past, when I was lost with Daniel in central London.

Oh Allah. I'm really worried about Mrs Hutchinson. Can you help me find her please? And can you make her be OK? I don't even mind being wrong about the alien stuff, because that would mean that poor Mrs H wouldn't have had to go through something so bad. Thank you, Allah. *Ameen.'*

Mum and Dad were calling us just then, because we were going to go shopping and then to visit some other relatives. Dad was holding one of the bags of chocolate in his hand.

In the car, he passed over some money for me, and some for Maryam, to spend at the shops.

'I don't know what you'll find, other than ladies' clothes and jewellery, but enjoy it anyway,' he winked.

He was right. There were rows and rows of men selling colourful fabrics for ladies to have their clothes sewn. Apparently, that's the way most people do it in Pakistan, instead of buying ready-made clothes. Some ladies sounded like they were arguing with the stall holders. Mum said they were haggling for the price, which is also the normal way to shop.

'So, you want to try to give them less money than they're asking for?' I said.

'Basically, yes,' said Mum.

'**But that's not fair**. They look poor,' I said.

'Well, they know you'll do it, so they ask for much more than it's worth anyway,' explained Mum.

I liked how busy it was, and how colourful. Everyone seemed to be enjoying themselves. We stopped at the stall of one man who only had hair around the sides of his head, but he had grown it long from one side and combed it over the top of his head, as some sort of baldness disguise. As Mum haggled with him over the price of fabric, the wind blew and the unfortunate hair flapped upwards, revealing the man's **NoT-So-SECRET SECRET**.

'700 rupees. Bas,' said the man, being firm and serious. But his hair wouldn't sit back down, it was like a flag flapping around at the top of a big, shiny mast.

It was such a funny sight, I wanted to burst out laughing. But I was controlling it the best I could, trying to look anywhere else but his head. It wasn't working. The hilarious hair was all my eyes would look at. I tried not to glance at Maryam, because I knew if I did and she was trying not to laugh as well, I would be able to tell, and then I would lose control.

Mum quickly gave in, handed him the cash and sped away, as Maryam and I slapped our hands over our giggles.

I hadn't forgotten to keep an eye out for Mrs Hutchinson. I thought I heard her voice for a minute, so I followed it, just a little away from where Mum and Dad were buying bangles for Mrs Rogers.

But when I got through the crowd of people and arrived at the human with the voice and tapped her shoulder, it wasn't Mrs H. And I was in BIG TROUBLE for walking off, because I had sent Mum and Dad into complete panic.

'OMAR! You NEVER walk away from us. NEVER. Especially in a city like LAHoRE!' screamed Mum frantically.

'Yeah, that was pretty stupid,' said Maryam.

'Were you looking for something to spend your money on?' asked Dad.

'Ermm, yes. I guess,' I said.

Mum insisted on holding my hand for a while, even though I'm not a baby like Esa. The shopping took ages, and it got **Super boring** after a while. We found a toy shop, and I stopped to look at some things, but instead, I gave my money to a poor lady on the floor who was rocking her baby.

CHAPTER 23

After shopping, we went to the house of our relatives, who were Dad's uncle's cousin's grandchildren, or something long like that. My uncle drove us there. He basically went everywhere with us, like a bodyguard or something.

There were a couple of goats outside their front door. Pakistan has lots of random animals like that. The relatives were grateful for the bag of chocolate. They looked as if they had just been given a bag of diamonds.

They kept asking Esa how old he was and what his name was and then cooing and gushing when he got it right.

Maryam whispered in my ear, 'He's *three*, he's not *dumb*. What's so impressive?'

I shrugged and tried to get through the funny food on my plate, which was way too full of chilli.

When it was time to leave, I was So Glad. I was looking forward to doing more fun stuff than shopping and visiting people's houses.

Dad asked if he could drive on the way back.

'Are you sure, darling?' Mum asked.

'The traffic here is bonkers.'

'Nothing I can't handle,' said Dad.

He was right. He wove in and out of the crazy, jumpy cars and tooted his horn for no reason, just like everyone else was doing.

I had my eyes peeled, making sure he didn't hit a donkey or a rickshaw. It was lots of fun. Like some sort of video game, where you had to drive along avoiding the obstacles and collecting points. I imagined the red cars were points if Dad overtook them, and the black cars were villains.

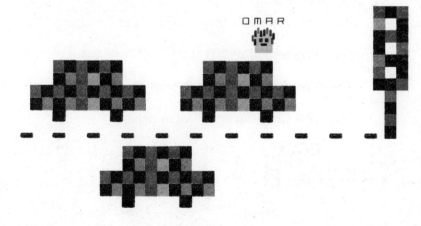

Then, as I was looking at everything on the road, Mrs Hutchinson's face appeared at the window of the same black Toyota I had seen at the restaurant. Her head was turned towards me, but she was looking right past me.

'OH MY GOD!

It's Mrs Hutchinson!' I shouted.

'Not again,' said Mum right away.

'Where?' said Maryam.

The Toyota had overtaken us. I could see it slightly up ahead. In a panic, I screamed, 'Dad! Follow that black Toyota!'

'Omar! No!' said Mum.

'Are you certain?' asked Dad.

'Yes!' I screamed again.

'**Listen to him!**' shouted Maryam.

'Don't listen to them, darling!' shouted Mum.

My uncle was making Urdu comments that I didn't understand, but the hand motions seemed to say, 'Omar is crazy for sure and why are you all shouting?'

'I have to help him!' shouted Dad, and stepped on the accelerator so hard, everyone's heads hit their headrests.

'**YESSSSSS DAD! YOU'RE THE BESSSSST!**'

Dad was on the Toyota's tail in seconds, just like I knew he would be, but there was a traffic light coming up and it went red. Dad sped through it anyway.

'What are you doing???!!' yelped Mum.

'Look around, nobody stops at the reds around here,' said Dad, jumping lanes and cutting in close in front of a white Audi to get behind the Toyota.

'You're as nuts as your kids,' said Mum, but I could tell she was enjoying the excitement, and she was beginning to smile and trying to hide it.

'Daddy is so fast!' laughed Esa.

The black Toyota took a left. Dad took the left. Then it took a right, Dad took it too, but he just skimmed a fruit stall on the corner, where someone had just piled up a load of apples in a pyramid, sending them tumbling down behind us.

'Oh bananas!!!' said Dad, looking in his mirrors. 'I have to stop and sort that out.'

'NOOOOOOOOO,' said Mum, to my utter surprise. 'We'll go back to him and help him later!'

YES! I knew Mum had it in her.

We were on the Toyota's heels again, travelling down a long narrow road. It was going fast, as if it knew it was being chased.

'Maybe she thinks the aliens are chasing her, or the FBI,' I said to Maryam.

Suddenly, the Toyota turned into the gates of a house. We parked up outside. I held my breath for what felt like ages, for the moment that would reveal everything. Waiting for her to step out of the car ...

CHAPTER 24

We all stared at the black Toyota. The driver stepped out first, then an older man and eventually the door I had been watching opened slowly, and out stepped my wonderful teacher.

'See! See! It's her!' I said.

PHEW! I didn't look silly in front of my family again. Everyone knew that bouncy, springy hair. It was Mrs H all right. No doubt about it.

'Let's go,' I said, one leg already out of the car door.

'We can't very well just go and knock on the door,' said Mum, too polite as always.

'Yes, we jolly well can,' said Dad. 'Let's put this thing to bed, eh?'

So, we did.

Mrs Hutchinson was shocked. **'Omar?! What on earth are you doing here?'**

I loved seeing her hair expressing more shock than her words, moving magically right before my eyes.

'What are **YOU** doing here?' I asked.

'Well, I guess I never told you this, but this is my husband,' she explained, gesturing to the bewildered-looking man beside her. The driver of the black Toyota. 'My husband is Pakistani,

like you, Omar. We're here for a break.'

WOW.

We all sat down with a cup of tea and some samosas and I told Mrs Hutchinson everything. Right from the start, blushing over at my parents every now and then, because they didn't know the half of it.

A couple of times, Mum wanted to jump in to say she couldn't believe all this was going on, but I saw Dad put a hand on her knee, to tell her to keep it in for now.

Mrs Hutchinson had listened very carefully, sometimes with shock and sometimes with amusement. But she didn't interrupt. She just let me finish.

'And ... well ... is that it?' I pointed to the bump that was her tummy. 'Is that the alien?'

'Well,' Mrs H spoke slowly, as if she was choosing her words carefully. 'It is a baby, but it's not an alien. It's my baby. I'm having a baby, Omar. A regular human one, I might add!'

She explained that she had to leave her job unexpectedly when she started feeling terribly sick because of the pregnancy and couldn't stop vomiting. She had left a letter with the school receptionist to be read out to the class, but it must have been overlooked. So, the conversation I overheard in the staffroom was about a real baby, not an alien baby.

The stack of post in the porch had gathered because Mrs H was away, but she was away *by choice.* She hadn't been abducted. The strange circles on her grass were from removing plant pots that had sat there for months, making the grass under them a different colour.

I asked her about the alien-in-disguise creature. 'We saw a really strange creature, though, which looked like an inside-out cat.'

'Oh,' chuckled Mrs H. 'That *is* a cat. My cat Seb. I think he's cute, though I know hairless cats aren't everyone's cup of tea.' She pulled out her phone and proudly showed us a picture of him.

'But what about the emails? Saying they saw you being taken by aliens?' I asked. A teeny, tiny part of me still believed I was right, and Mrs H was hiding it all from us.

'I'm afraid somebody might have seen your posters and was pulling your leg, Omar.'

'Oh ...'

Mrs H was touched, nonetheless. She couldn't believe her students cared about her so much.

'I did hate to be away from you all,' she sighed.

I gave her a big hug. I know you don't really hug teachers, but here in Pakistan in these crazy circumstances it felt like the right thing to do. I guess I hadn't imagined seeing her, but I had let my imagination make up a more exciting story from the clues we had found. Oops.

CHAPTER 25

I was allowed to call Charlie and Daniel to tell them everything that had happened. I sent them a message first to ask them to meet up, so I could tell them together.

'That's the CRAZIEST STORY I ever heard! What are the chances?' said Charlie.

'Well, apparently better chances than her being taken by aliens,' I admitted sheepishly.

'I *told* you guys it wasn't aliens!' said Daniel proudly.

'But what about those articles we read about there being aliens out there?' Charlie asked.

'Well, Dad said they found lifeforms, but that's not the same as actual green aliens that can walk and kidnap humans. It's just little bacteria or something puny like that.'

'Oh ... hahahaha.'

'But who sent us those emails? I'll get them!' said Daniel.

Charlie's eyes went wide. 'How can we not have guessed it? I bet it was Ellie and Sarah! They were always eavesdropping and asking questions!'

'Argh, I knew they were up to something!' I said.

'Hahaha, guess they got us this time!'

By the end of the conversation, we were in

hysterical fits of laughter

about it all.

'I'll see you guys when I get back in a couple of days!' I said.

I was desperate to see them to talk more about it. On the plane, it was all I could think of, instead of watching movies or doing puzzles.

I thought about the dinner we had had the evening before we flew back home. Mum had arranged for us to have a proper meal with Mrs Hutchinson and her husband. He was very nice, and actually reminded me of Dad quite a lot.

No wonder he was driving fast that day!

I thought about the time when I was new in

class and **nobody knew it was Ramadan,**

but Mrs H did. I guessed it was probably

because of him, which made me like him more.

When we finally arrived back at our front

door, I was so happy. There's no place like your

own home. Even though we had had lots of fun

and had finally solved

Operation Moon Dust.

Mrs Rogers was glad to have us back too.

She loved all the gifts we got her:

- a purple woollen shawl to stay warm
- a Pakistani outfit
- matching bangles with the outfit

I got Charlie and Daniel some stickers and

postcards with funny things written on them,

and some keyrings that said,

I ♥ PAKISTAN

I even got Mrs Crankshaw

a scarf, because Mum said it

would be a **a nice gesture.**

On my first day back at school, I wrapped it in pink tissue paper and put it in my bag to give to her.

I didn't run in through the school gates like I normally do when I haven't seen my friends for a while. I was glad Mrs Hutchinson was OK, but still super sad that she wasn't our teacher any more. I wondered what boring things Mrs C would have in store for us today.

I saw Daniel and Charlie doing the same sad walk as I was to our line in the playground. Though we cheered up a bit when I told them both more about my adventure, especially the car chase.

Daniel suddenly got a funny look on his face. He quickly walked away and came back with a stubborn-looking Sarah and Ellie. 'Tell them,' he said.

The girls looked like they had won and were very pleased with themselves. 'It was us who sent you those emails and we're sorry.' They didn't *sound* sorry, not one bit.

'You'll be sorry when I make you eat avocadoes!' said Daniel.

Charlie and I laughed and put our arms around Daniel. 'It's OK,' we said. 'It was quite funny, actually.'

The bell rang and we all braced ourselves for another day with Mrs CrankyForSure.

But when the teacher came out to get us, it wasn't her ... it was Mrs Hutchinson! In all her bouncy hair glory!

The time away and some special medicines

apparently made her feel a lot better, so she was able to come back and be our teacher again until her baby arrived.

It was the BEST DAY ever!

'Will you give Mrs H the scarf instead?' asked Charlie.

I thought about it for a bit.

'No, I think Mrs Crankshaw probably needs something to help her stop being so grumpy,' I smiled. 'I'll post it to her.'

And I did.

ZANIB MIAN grew up in London and still
lives there today. She was a science teacher for
a few years after leaving university but, right
from when she was a little girl, her passion was
writing stories and poetry. She has released lots
of picture books with the independent publisher
Sweet Apple Publishers, but the *Planet Omar*
series is the first time she's written for older
readers.

NASAYA MAFARIDIK is based in Indonesia. Self-taught, she has a passion for books and bright, colourful stationery.

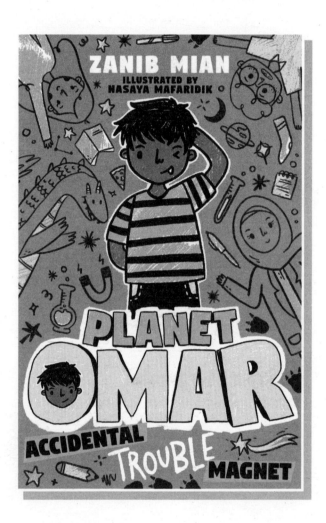

ZANIB MIAN

ILLUSTRATED BY
NASAYA MAFARIDIK

PLANET OMAR

ACCIDENTAL TROUBLE MAGNET